"At this time London was agog with the exploits of Jack the Ripper.
One theory of the motive of the murderer was that he was performing
an Operation to obtain the Supreme Black Magical Power."

— THE CONFESSIONS OF ALEISTER CROWLEY
edited by JOHN SYMONDS & KENNETH GRANT
(Routledge & Keegan Paul, 1979)

"Blood is the great materializing agent, both for spirits that would incarnate in
this world (or on this plane) and for spirits which, remaining in another world,
wish to assume a shape in order to impress their presence upon human beings."

— THE MAGICAL REVIVAL
by KENNETH GRANT
(Frederick Muller, Ltd., 1972)

"'I win!' shouted Fantomas, as a terrible explosion sounded. The earth shook, a
huge column of black smoke rose skyward, and explosion followed explosion.
The roar of walls collapsing was mingled with fearful cries and dying groans."

— THE SILENT EXECUTIONER
by MARCEL ALLAIN & PIERRE SOUVESTRE
(Pan Books, Ltd., 1988)

writer ALAN MOORE • artist EDDIE CAMPBELL

art assistance PETE MULLINS • logo TODD KLEIN • chapter heading calligraphy DES RODEN
design and production MICHAEL EASTMAN, KEVIN LISON, BRENDAN STEPHENS
editor PHILIP AMARA • art director TAMARA SIBERT

publisher DENIS KITCHEN • vp-deputy publisher JUDITH HANSEN • vp-production JIM KITCHEN
vp-business affairs and merchandising SCOTT HYMAN • sales and marketing director JAMIE RIEHLE
sales manager GAIL "ZIGGY" ZYGMONT • controller KIM HASTINGS
customer service manager KAREN LOWMAN • warehouse managers JOHN WILLS & VIC LISEWSKI

Chapter Nine

From Hell

Mitre Square; Sunday, September 30th, 1888

Mitre Square, Ladies and Gents. Mitre Square...

'Ave you ever seen a spot upon this Earth so Cursed?

Yes, that's right, madam! I said CURSED! Cursed since the Sixteenth Century, when the Priory of the Holy Trinity stood where you stand now!

Imagine it, if you will, Ladies; The year is 1530. A young woman kneels there at the Priory altar, bent in prayer...

Suddenly, she's struck down!

MURDERED at her devotions, Gentleman, by an INSANE MONK...

... whose likeness is carved on these WALKING STICKS and whose tale is recounted in this PAMPHLET!

Now the curse has struck again, who can refuse these lovely souvenirs at only sixpence ha'penny the pair? Just the stick, sir? That'll be sixpence.

Well, he *seems* to be turning a fair trade, sir. Ever heard of it, that other murder he mentioned?

No, Godley, I 'aven't... and I doubt 'E 'as either.

It's all a load of tom, shifting a few old walking sticks off the back of some poor murdered tart. And 'er barely cold. Makes me sick.

You don't go much on this "curse" business, then?

No, nor mad monks neither, nor with turning a miserable little killing into a Gothic horror!

I mean, just *LOOK* at 'em back there; Four women get killed and it's like the start of a new *INDUSTRY!* Only the start, mind you.

Mark my words, in 'undred years there'll still be cunts like 'im, wrapping these killings up in supernatural twaddle, making a living out of murder, Godley...

...and that's *OUR* job. Let's drop by the Golden Lane Mortuary, shall we? For the post-mortem?

From Hell, chapter 9, page 2

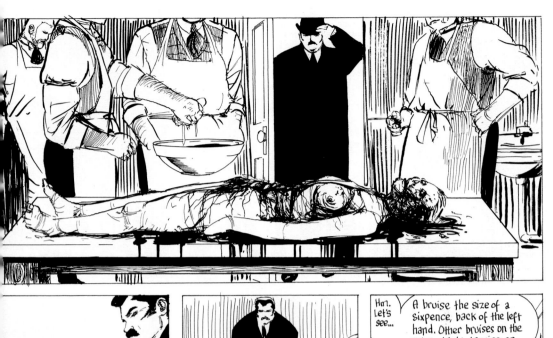

Hm. Let's see...

A bruise the size of a sixpence, back of the left hand. Other bruises on the shins. Light tanning on arms and legs.

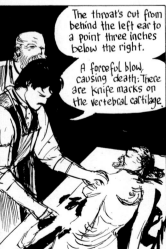

The throat's cut from behind the left ear to a point three inches below the right.

A forceful blow, causing death. There are knife marks on the vertebral cartilage.

The abdomen is laid open from pubes to sternum in an upward cut, a rip.

He was probably kneeling to the right of the body.

It's 'er, sir. Me sister, Elizabeth Watts. Night she died, I dreamed she visited me.

Mrs. Malcolm, your sister contacted us recently. You are mistaken. Next witness.

Ya. This is Elizabeth Stride, I think, from Gothenburg in Sweden. As Elizabeth Gustafsdotter I KNEW her.

Thank you, Pastor Ollson. Shall we retire to the vestry?

There. Now reports that the deceased lost her family in 1878's Princess Alice disaster seem unfounded. No corroboration exists. Let us proceed to her final night.

...saw 'er leavin' the Bricklayer's Arms with this chap, 'uggin' an' kissin'. We chaffed 'em a bit, they was off like a shot. Just after eleven, it was.

P.C. Smith, sir, 452 H. At 12.30 A.M. I saw the deceased in Berner Street with a man aged about 28. He was dark; about 5 foot 7; small, dark moustache...

...stood opposite my 'ouse in Berner Street with this bloke. Peaked sailor cap, 'e 'ad on. Quarter to midnight, this was. I 'eard 'im say summat to 'er...

Ha! You'd say anythin' but your prayers.

..concludes our inquest for today, ladies and gentlemen. We shall reconvene tomorrow. A very good day to you all.

No mention of organ dealers. Baxter most've had his knuckles rapped.

Hm. They never called that fruiterer, Packer, or Schwartz, who saw 'er attacked...

Inspector Abberline?

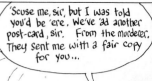

'Scuse me, sir, but I was told you'd be 'ere. We've 'ad another post-card, sir. From the murderer. They sent me with a fair copy for you...

Oh, fuckin' 'ell.

"I was not codding dear old Boss when I gave you the tip. You'll hear about saucy Jacky's work tomorrow double event this time..."

POST CARD

"Number one squealed a bit couldn't finish straight off. Had not time to get ears for police thanks for keeping last letter back till I go to work again"

"Jack the Ripper" Well, the papers are gunna love this, ain't they? Lap it up, they will. I wonder what 'e's doin' now, the cunt who wrote this.

I wonder where 'e is.

We would hear again, Sir William, of the necessity for such excessive ghastliness in these eliminations.

You say these mutilations were a "warning", but to whom?

To certain enemies of Freemasonry, your majesty, The scourge of ILLUMINISM has reached England via a recently founded order called "The Golden Dawn"

These... "demonstrations"... may have kept it in check.

Sir William, you were asked to remove a threat to our throne and family. We gave no further sanction.

Of what concern is Illuminism to the crown?

With respect, your majesty, it is of the gravest concern. This country has thus far been free of Bavarian Illuminism.

Other countries, however, have been infiltrated.

France, for example.

Just prior to its revolution.

Ahh. We understand. Very well, Sir William. It appears that you know better than we. Go forth with our blessing.

Thank you, your majesty

Uh, excuse me? Sir William? Sir William Gull?

Um?

If you'll forgive me, sir, I am Robert Lees, psychic adviser to her majesty. I am familiar with you work, sir, and have long anticipated this meeting.

Indeed? I am similarly familiar with YOUR work, sir, profiting from delusions born of bereavement.
Consequently, I have relished this meeting not at all. Good day.

From Hell. Chapter 9. page 12.

Sir William. We are honoured, sir, deeply honoured by your visit.
I am at your disposal, sir. If there is anything with which I can assist...

Let us hope so.
There is in England a mummy-case from Thebes currently in private hands. Does the British Museum intend to purchase it?

Ah, yes, yes, I have heard of the, ah, of the item. Excellent piece. First class. Of course, there IS the matter of its, ah reputation, so to speak...

For shame! Do we approach the twentieth century beset yet by such chimaera, that pagan curses daunt this noble institution?

I-It's not that, sir. It's...

Think of it, man! What better place for such an artefact than here in this museum, next to Hawksmoor's Bloomsbury Church? Shall superstition weigh against good policy?

Half London's mad for things Egyptian with the Royal Household held alike in thrall. It is, sir, an unconscionable oversight.

I-I'll see to it, sir.

Excellent. Then I shall not trouble you further. I take it that your Blake exhibits are still in the same location?

Yes, sir, th- thank you, sir.

Excuse me, sir...

...but would I be addressing Mr. William Yeats?

Yes?

Splendid. I am Sir William Gull. I fancied I had seen you before, In the company of Dr. Westcott.

How is Westcott's little group, by the way?

If you refer to The Order of the Golden Dawn, then we are far from "little", sir.

You are a splinter, split from the bough of Masonry...

...no longer nourished by its truths nor anchored by the roots of its tradition, soon to wither.

The older ways have yet more blood in them.

Say what you will, sir. You are welcome to remain ensconced in lore and ritual. For my part I am happy to entertain a questioning spirit.

Ha ha ha! Then mark my words, Mr. Yeats, your bones shall never rest easy.

Good day to you, sir.

From Hell Chapter 9 page 15.

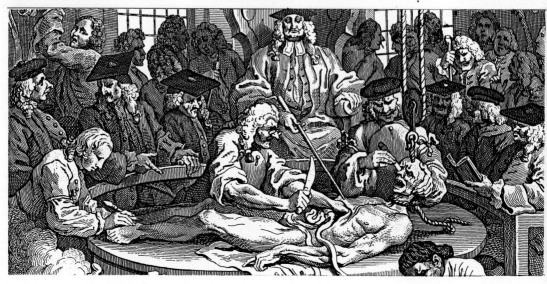

Joe?

Joe, is th'r anymore in the paper about the murders now? Joe? D'ye hear me? I said...

I heard what ye said, and no, there isn't, not since the last time ye asked. Donno what yer so stuck with 'em for.

Why shouldn't I be?

Because there's other things want doin'! You should pull yourself together and get dressed.

I thought ye liked me this way best. I thought ye liked me undressed.

Penny for them, old bean.

Hm?
Oh, I was just thinking how nice it was that you'd kept these rooms at Neville's Court, Jem. They hold such happy memories of Cambridge.

Ah yes, the dear old Cambridge Attics. Remember the Apostles Society meeting here? Old Harry Wilson, Ronnie Gower and all the rest? What times?

Yes, it was all so much jollier then, wasn't it? One never heard about... well, all these dreadful things.

Oh, Eddie, you're not still brooding about those wretched MURDERS?

How can I HELP it, Jem? TWO more women, were killed last WEEK...

Huh. Women. The Apostles ideal was the Higher Sodomy, remember? The pure love between fellows?

You take this latest poem of mine for example...
"If all the harm that women have done were put in a bundle and rolled into one Earth would not hold it, The sky could not enfold it...

"Such masses of evil would puzzle the devil And keep him in fuel while Time's wheels run."

I'm sure it's terribly good, Jem, but I'm not in the mood.

I'd hoped I could shake off this beastly fit by visiting you, but I can't.

I-I return to London in a month. Perhaps I can do something then.

...although what can I do? Nobody tells me anything; they won't let me have a say, and... Jem?

J-Jem? What are you...?

Shh, I want to gamahuche you, Eddie. Do say I might.

Jem, I... I don't think we should. It's not... I mean, I... oh God

Oh God, Jem... Jem, I'm so weak. I-I'm not bad...

Just weak.

GOLDEN LANE

From Hell Chapter 9 - page 20.

:just told you! I'm investigating this ase and I need to tend the inquest.

And I've told you this is CITY police business, committed within city jurisdiction.

Alright, what's all this then?

He says the Met aren't allowed. Says it's City business. I've told the silly bugger till I'm blue in the face, but...

That's enough, Godley.

I'm Inspector Abberline, Scotland Yard. The City Commissioner, Major Smith, approved our visit.

oh well, that's different, sir. my apologies. Please go straight in.

Jumped up little pillock. Good job you bothered to get Major Smith's permission.

I didn't. Now shut up and let's find a seat.

...that you are John Kelly, and lived with the deceased at 55 Flower and Dean st.

That's right, sir. Yes. N-Nearly seven years we lived there.

Hmm. "Kelly". S'probably why she gave the name Kelly to the police earlier.

very likely. Now 'ush, I'm listenin'.

I last saw her Saturday in Houndsditch.

She said she'd go to her daughter's in Bermondsey. Later, I heard she'd been locked up drunk, and then...

Yes, Thank you, mr. Kelly. Next Witness, please.

Dr. Brown, you conducted the post mortem on the deceased. Would you consider that the person who inflicted the wounds possessed great anatomical skill.?

A great deal of knowledge as to the position of the organs in the abdominal cavity... and the way of removing them.

Ay c'mon. I was only tryin' to 'elp.

Oh, I know. I'm sorry, Fred, I'm sorry. It's just ye've been so good t'me...

Aye, well, look, I couldn't do it till the first o' next month, but I could lend you the money.

Oh, Fred, I can't take...

Now you shush a minute. It'd only be a loan. You could pay me back.

Oh, Fred, it'd be within the week, I promise. Are ye sure?

Course I am.

Oh, Fred, ye don't know, ye don't know what this means. God, if you weren't a married man!

Tch. Godley, will you get your fuckin' great feet off my desk?!

Whups. Sorry, guv.

TUESDAY
9 OCT

You fuckin' will be, lad. Any news while I was out?

Well, apparently Commissioner Warren volunteered to be tracked by bloodhounds.

'e did WHAT?

Two bloodhounds, sir, Barnaby and Burgho. It's his new idea for catching the murderer.

Anyway, he tried them out the other day...

Good God, as if we didn't look fuckin' silly enough already. I 'ope 'e did it somewhere PRIVATE.

Hyde Park, sir.

HYDE PARK? Did anybody see 'im?

Well, only all the newspaper reporters he'd invited along.

Here, have a look; it's on the front page.

Christ almighty.

Inspecting the dogs

cry

At Fault

Crossing the scent

Inspector Abber'line? I'm Lees, Robert James Lees. I called yesterday, but they wouldn't let me see you.

We ARE very busy, sir...

Too busy to catch the Whitechapel killer? I think not, Inspector.

You see, I have... certain talents. Her majesty has made use of me upon occasion.

I'm sure she 'as, sir.

I'm Psychic, you see. Just recently, I've been subjected to fearful intimations of the murderer's movements ...even his very IDENTITY

You're sayin' you know 'oo the murderer is?

N-not EXACTLY. my clairvoyant senses tell me that he's a very well-placed man socially... possibly a DOCTOR.

I see. And when did you receive these... clairvoyant impressions?

Inspector I beg you!.. Do not make me RECALL them! They were too horrible...

well, if you'd rather not...

No. No. I must steel myself. It began with the last murder. Alone in my study, I seemed to SEE the events happening...

It— I didn't ACT on my vision, but then recently, my wife and I were riding in a London Omnibus.

Atop Notting Hill, a-a MAN got on...

SANITAS DISINFECTANT SOAPS FOR ALL PURPOSES

ZEBRA GRATE POLISH.

I told my wife "That's Jack the Ripper." She laughed. I said that I was not mistaken, that I FELT it.

He dismounted at Marble Arch. I FOLLOWED him...

Halfway down Oxford Street, certain of myself, I alerted a CONSTABLE. I indicated the man and revealed who he WAS. H-he LAUGHED, Inspector. The constable LAUGHED.

H-he even threatened to ARREST me. By then, the killer had escaped by CAB down PICADILLY.

Bad luck, sir. Well, if you see im again, you let us know.

You don't BELIEVE me, do you?

Well, to be perfectly frank, sir...

You'll be sorry! When more blood's spilled, you'll be sorry you didn't LISTEN! Goodbye, Inspector.

And so, mr. Pizer, you are also known as "Leather Apron", is that correct?

Well, according to Sergeant Thick I am, sir. yes.

I see, and yet we have had testimony from a police officer that he spoke with you on August 31st. This was when the Nichols girl was murdered?

Yes, sir, about half-past one, it was, down the Seven Sisters Road. I chatted with a copper about the red glow in the sky.

This was from the fire a't Ratcliffe docks?

Yessir. On my life, I never knew I was called "Leather Apron" until Thick told me I was.

The simple fact of your being elsewhere at the time of the murder is enough to demonstrate your innocence. Your are cleared of all suspicion.

Sergeant Thick, who arrested me, has known me for eighteen years.

Well, well, I do not think it is necessary for you to say more.

Instead, let us move on to the next witness. Call Sergeant William Thick...

Whore's gets. Fucking whore's gets.

You are Police Sergeant William Thick of H.Division, warrant no 49889, responsible for the arrest of John Pizer

That's right, sir, yessir.

On the tenth of September, having identified him with the suspect, "Leather Apron", you arrested John Pizer, am I correct?

Sergeant Thick?

Uh, yessir. I've known Mr. Pizer for many years and, uh...

Well, when people in the neighbourhood talked about "Leather Apron", they meant him.

I see.

Well, in that case, I think we may as well move along...

Why, even I'm regarded by the press and public as a sexual murderer!

Had I killed artists and not whores, should I be an ARTISTIC murderer? Pah!

It ANGERS me. And now, the wrong girl slain; the rightful victim still at large.

Ahh, this is Hell make no mistake.

It is the Hell of Faustus in a work I late admired but recently have put aside.

It is the volume's end; of late it troubles me.

'Tis Dante I prefer. In his INFERNO, he suggests the one true path from Hell lies at its very heart...

...and that in order to escape, we must instead go further IN.

With purpose thus renewed let us confront our persecutors.

Newsmen mock us with their "Jack the Ripper" jibes. Let us mock newsmen in return!

Let us reclaim from them the myth they sought to shape for profit.

Let us give them truer legends, grand enough to slake their morbid thirsts.

Let us acquaint these fabricators with reality.

Tell me now, Netley; Can you write?

W-well, it's the same as me readin', sir. It's not much good, like.

Excellent! That furnishes us with the touch of bedlam we require. Do you possess materials for writing?

Over on the side there, sir, but...

Splendid!

Then you shall write whilst I dictate. We're going to write a letter, Netley.

A letter? 'Oo to?

Oh, Mr. Lusk, perhaps, or his Whitechapel Vigilance Committee.

I wonder, Netley... how would you begin a missive of this kind?

Oh, well... I suppose I'd put "Dear Mr. Lusk", sir...

Oh, come, now. Are you not aware that one begins a letter with one's own address?

"From Hell", Netley. Write that down.

From Hell.

Well, it's a real kidney, Godley. Whether it belongs to the Eddowes woman or not, I dunno.

Lusk received it on October sixteenth.

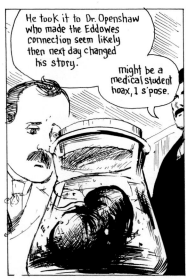

He took it to Dr. Openshaw who made the Eddowes connection seem likely then next day changed his story.

Might be a medical student hoax, I s'pose.

Mind you, the length of the artery matches what was left in Eddowes body.

I dunno, Godley. This whole fuckin' business.

I mean, 'ow many letters allegedly from or about the killer 'ave we 'ad now? Dozens? 'Undreds?

I know.

There was that Dr. Winslow who got this one recently from some prophet called "Lunigi":

Said the next murder would be November 8th or 9th.

Huh, and there's old Anderson writin' to the 'Ome office sayin' 'ow EXTRAORDINARY it is, all these murders an' us without a clue.

We've nothin' BUT clues.

We're BURIED under clues! If I could get my 'ands on the blokes 'oo wrote this "Jack the Ripper" tripe.

Not just blokes, sir. They caught a woman in Bradford writing letters pretending to be the murderer.

Hm, she's probably the exception, though. Not the rule.

I mean, what kind of men, Godley? What kind of men write stuff like this?

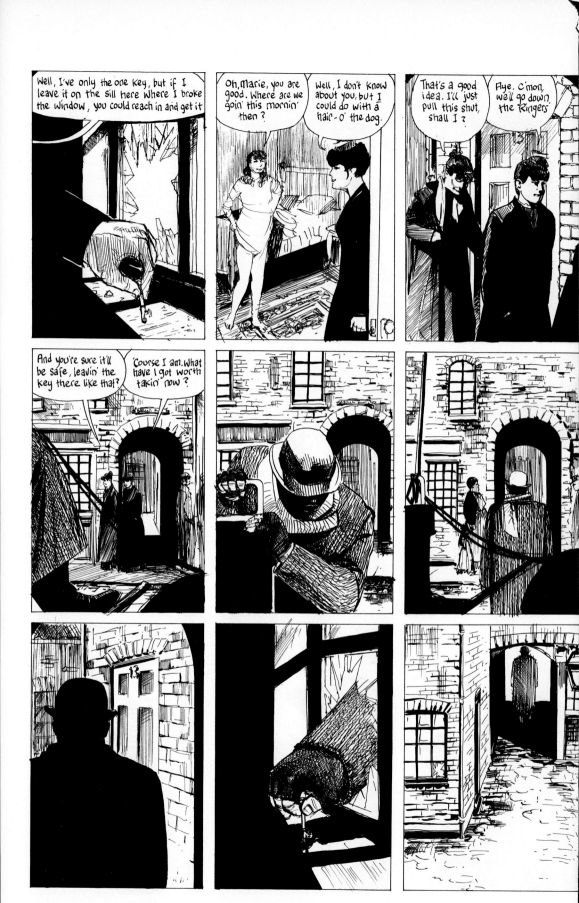

I'm sorry I could not attend Your Highness when you arrived from York yesterday. Sandringham next, isn't it?

Ah well, I'm relieved to say that everything is in order.

...thought I had detected a sarcocele, but it was merely a blemish.

Still, I would respectfully suggest your Highness be discriminate in such liaisons.

Yes. Yes, I suppose I should. My affairs do rather tend to get people into trouble, don't they?

Do you remember Annie Crook, Sir William?

Hm? Ahh, yes. The Crook woman. What a hornet's nest she stirred up. But no matter. That will all be concluded shortly.

C-concluded? You mean... those women? The Blackmail attempt?

Please, your Highness, a little softer. There are footmen.

But to answer your question: yes, I have recently located the remaining woman in Dorset Street, Whitechapel.

So have no fear, Your Highness.

There are seven days remaining until the Lord Mayor's Parade. By then this grave embarrassment shall be no more.

You have my oath.

Penny for the Guy, mate?

Clear off! Bonfire night's ages away

It ent. It's next Monday. C'mon, don't you wanna look a toff for the lady.

Ha Ha, Go on, Fred. Don't be tight.

Huh, 'Ere y'are, then. Now let us by afore I clip yer ear.

Cuh! Ta, mate.

Cheeky little buggers.

Ah, ye say that, but ye've a kind heart underneath it.

Ark 'oo's talkin'! Didn't you tell me not five minutes ago you'd taken some 'omeless woman in, when you can 'ardly feed yourself?

'Ere y'are. In here.

Aye, well, that's different. That don't cost me nothin'. But what you're doin' for me...

C'mon, Emm, let's not start it again. What'll yo 'ave to drink.

Marie? Are ye home? It's me, Julia. I see you've not found that key yet, then.

Oh, listen, you should have seen all the bonfires tonight.

They had ever such a big one up at London Fields. I... oh.

Come on in, now. This is Maria Harvey. Maria, this is Julia, who I said about.

Will you join us, Julia? It'll be a bit of fun.

No... no, it's all right I'll be comfortable down here.

Well, if ye're sure.

It's like when me first husband died, in that pit-accident. All that week, things had a feelin' to them. D'ye know what I mean?

I can't say I do. Look, shall we go and buy that candle or what?

Alright, I'm comin'. It was like things had a pattern I couldn't quite see.

It's like there was a kind of lace tyin' things together. A kind of lace over everything.

Lace? What do you mean? God, you have some bloody funny ideas sometimes, Marie Kelly.

Huh, you sound just like Joe. He used t'say that.

Are you missin' him?

It's been a week. I keep thinkin' I might never see him again. Oh well, enough o' that. Let's get this candle!

Huh! Marie Kelly, 'ow dare you show your face in 'ere, owin' me all that rent.

Oh, come on, Mr. McCarthy! Ye know ye'll get it. I'm after a ha'penny candle.

Hoho! "Here comes a candle to light you to bed", ay?

Aye! or "Here comes a chopper to chop off your-"

Maria, don't.

Don't say that.

C'mon. We ought t'be goin'. I don't like leavin' the house with nobody there.

It's havin' the window broke like that does it, and not bein' able to fix it. God, I wish I could remember where I put that key.

From Hell Chapter 9 - page 50.

Oh, undoubtedly. But you're helpless.

The final removal shall occur tonight. See... I have the young lady's door key.

What mysteries, Warren? What mysteries might this 'unlock'?

Gull, please, Don't. It's the Lord Mayor's Parade tomorrow. It's an important Masonic event.

So is this. A very good night to you, Sir Charles.

Cutbush? Send a stenographer to my office, would you? I need to dictate a letter.

Yes, sir? Concerning what, sir?

my resignation.

13 oh it's you.

Aye. I thought I'd call by, but if I'm interruptin'...

You're not, Joe. This is Lizzie.

Don't mind me. I'm just off. It's nearly eight.

You don't have to go because o' me.

Oh it's not that. I'm expected. See you presently, Marie.

Goodbye, Lizzie.

So... You're alright, then. I thought perhaps we could have a drink later.

Mm. I'm meetin' Julia in The Horn o' Plenty soon. Come along.

Aye. Aye, perhaps just for a quick one. And after that, like? Are ye doin' anything tomorrow?

I hope so

THE HORN O' PLENTY

Marie Kelly? Is that you makin' the noise? It's nearly quarter to midnight.

Oh, hello, Mrs. Cox. We're just goin' to have a sing-song, aren't we, m'love.

Mm.

From Hell - Chapter 9 - page 56.

From Hell - Chapter 9 - page 58.

A P P E N D I X

PAGES 1 & 2

The legend of the mad monk of Mitre Square, as recounted by the salesman here, was one in popular currency at the time of the murder and is related in Stephen Knight's *JTR: The Final Solution*. Since no historical record relates the alleged events of 1530 actually taking place, it seems likely that the story is a form of urban legend, revived and exploited in the wake of the Mitre Square murders by salesmen and pamphleteers of the type depicted here. Decorated walking sticks and pamphlets detailing the mad monk's exploits were on sale in Mitre Square shortly after the murders, although in fairness, they probably didn't appear the very next day as suggested here, this being merely a convenience of fiction. The design of the walking sticks relates to events in subsequent chapters of *From Hell* and will be dealt with in the relevant appendix. Abberline's eerily precognitive comments on page two are my own invention. They are also, in their way, a form of shamefaced apology from one currently making part of his living wrapping up miserable little killings in supernatural twaddle. Sometimes, after all you've done for them, your characters just turn on you.

PAGES 3 & 4

The crowds in Golden Lane on the morning after the murders are according to numerous commentators, with Paul Begg adding in *Jack the Ripper, The Uncensored Facts* that additional police were brought in to protect the mortuary.

Abberline's meeting with the young Alexander Crowley (who later changed his name to Aleister for largely numerological reasons when he discovered that the letters in "Alexander" only added up to the second cousin of the Beast) is an invention. According to Crowley's autobiography, *The Confessions of Aleister Crowley* edited by John Symonds and Kenneth Grant (Routledge & Keegan Paul, 1979), Crowley moved with his mother to London in 1887 when he was thirteen. Given that in later life he showed more than a passing interest in the Whitechapel murders, it seemed possible that he may have been drawn to them as a spectator during his childhood. His own contradiction to Ripperology was an essay in which he accused Madame Blavatsky, leader of the Theosophists, of the murders. He also turns up as a theorist and informant in various books of Ripper lore, most notably in Stephen Knight's *JTR: The Final Solution*, where reference is made to one of Crowley's books, *The World's Tragedy* (Paris, 1910). In this tome, Crowley alleges that he is in receipt of a number of letters written by Prince Eddie to a young boy residing at the sweetshop in Cleveland Street where we saw Annie Crook working in Chapter One.

In light of these connections, the opportunity to include a fairly spurious cameo by one of the foremost occultists of all time seemed too good to pass up. Young Alexander's suggestion that the murderer might be planning to make himself invisible by arranging his killing into a certain pattern was indeed one of the stranger theories put forward at the time, the pattern in question being the inevitable pentacle. Crowley's reference to it here is included purely because of its relevance to Crowley's later profession.

PAGES 5 & 6

The details of Catherine Eddowes' postmortem
are taken from various sources, the closest to
hand being the The Jack the Ripper A-Z by Begg,
Fido & Skinner. Paul Begg's JTR, The Uncensored
Facts details the disagreement between the various
doctors who attended the postmortem over
whether the murderer had possessed any surgical
skill or not. The details of the injuries discovered
during the postmortem as presented here are
according to the same sources.

PAGE 7

The rallies taking place all over London, and
the speech given by Mr. Lusk of the Whitechapel
Vigilance Committee that Abberline and Godley
mention here, are according to The JTR, The
Uncensored Facts by Paul Begg. The information
that Elizabeth Stride's inquest was conducted in
the Vestry Hall of Hawksmoor's St. George's-in-
the-East in Cable Street comes from The JTR A-Z
by Begg, Fido & Skinner. This was the same
location that the bodies of the similarly-mutilated
Ratcliffe Highway murder victims had been taken
to over seventy years before.

PAGES 8 - 10

The details of Liz Stride's inquest on pages
eight and nine are assembled from various
sources, most notably Jack The Ripper, Summing
Up And Verdict by Colin Wilson and Robin
Odell (Bantam Press, 1987). The postcard
delivered to Abberline on page ten can also be
found in the above publication, although it is
of course common to most of the books concerning the subject.

PAGE 11

Sir William Gull's conversation with Queen
Victoria here is an invention with only tenuous
links to reality, and is only included to give a
little background to some of the fears and phobias
preying on both the monarchy and organized
Freemasonry during this period. Queen Victoria,
throughout her lengthy reign, was haunted by
morbid fears of uprising and the guillotine-spectre
of revolutionary France. According to Stephen
Knight, Victoria had been worried since the
mid-1860s about the possibility of "a new French
Revolution" happening in England, and that fear
is reflected here. Gull's remarks about the
Bavarian Illuminati, while obviously intended as
a smoke screen to gain the queen's acquiescence
by exploiting her fears, are nevertheless based
upon a genuine unease prevalent amongst
Freemasons of the period. Adam Weishaupt's
Bavarian Illuminati can best be understood on one
level as a kind of Masonic bogeyman; a current of
paranoia running through Masonry at that time.
Since the avowed aim of the Illuminati had been
to infiltrate Masonry, many masons began to fall
prey to the same kind of fears that Freemasonry
itself often provokes in broad society, fears of an
invisible and clandestine organization working
covertly in its very midst. An Illuminati influence
was believed to be behind the revolutions that
had claimed France and America during the
eighteenth century. The Order of the Golden
Dawn, a prototypical version of which had come
into being during 1887, was said by the occultist
A.E. Waite, amongst others, to represent a
reformation of Weishaupt's original Bavarian
Illuminati, thus implying to some Freemasons that

A P P E N D I X

he invisible taint of Illuminism had finally
eached these shores and would shortly
recipitate a revolution. Alas, no such luck
s of this writing.

A G E 12

The scene here detailing the brief and frosty
meeting between Gull and Robert Lees
s intended to resolve a point that bothered me
n the account of Lee's involvement with the case
is recounted in *JTR: The Final Solution* and elsewhere. Lees, as will be seen in Chapter Twelve
of *From Hell*, claimed to have led the police to the
murderer's door following his psychic intuitions.
The murderer turned out to be a doctor living
n the West End who subsequent writers have
often identified as William Gull. Now, if one is
prepared to accept the validity of psychic
phenomena for a moment, this seems on the
surface at least plausible. The problem arises
when we consider that Robert Lees was allegedly
Queen Victoria's pet psychic during the same
period that William Gull was the Queen's
Physician in Ordinary. It seems unlikely that if
this were the case they would not have met,
and unlikelier still that Robert Lees would not
immediately recognize the famous physician when
glimpsing him while riding an omnibus, Lees
account of which is detailed later in this chapter.
If Lees had recognized Gull at first sight, then it
is difficult not to suspect malicious intent in the
act of leading the constabulary to Gull's front
door. I have attempted to resolve the issue with
the meeting depicted here, which is necessarily
an invention. Since even Gull's biographer
(and adoring son-in-law) reveals him as a

sardonically humorous man with a skill for verbal
wounding and an unwillingness to suffer fools
gladly, the exchange shown here does not seem
out of character. I shall return to the relationship
of Gull and Lees later in my notes upon this
current chapter.

P A G E S 13 - 15

Gull's visit to the British Museum is also an
invention, albeit not out of keeping with his de-
clared interests. The mummy case referred to is
that of the Theban court musician as discussed in
the appendix notes to Book Three, to which I
would refer the interested reader (I assume there's
only one of you). The reason for the scene's
inclusion is to make possible the fictional meeting
between William Gull and poet William Butler
Yeats as detailed on pages fourteen and fifteen.
According to most biographical sources, Yeats
was researching the life and work of William
Blake in the British Museum during the autumn of
the murders, and had just been inducted into the
Isi-Urania Temple (later the Order of the Golden
Dawn) during the previous year. Gull's remark
about Yeats' bones had additional significance in
light of what eventually happened to the
aforementioned relics: Yeats died in France and
was interred at an ossiery, where the bones are
stored according to the type of bone in question
rather than according to whom they originally
belonged to, so that there will be a room of
skulls, a room of femurs and so on. Imagine the
embarrassment of the French authorities, then,
when Yeats' family requested that his remains be
returned to Ireland, the land of his birth. A
skeleton *was* hurriedly assembled and shipped to

Ireland for burial with honours, but it was, in all likelihood, a Frankensteinian effort composited from a dozen separate donors. This information is according to *Gluck*, a biography of the eponymous gay woman artist for which I'm afraid I have no details pertaining to publisher or author available at the moment. The painting visible in the last panel on page fifteen is "The Ghost of a Flea" by William Blake, and has relevance to events in the final chapter of *From Hell*.

PAGE 16

This page is another invention for story purposes, the only point in need of explanation being the inclusion of the etching hanging on the wall of Gull's hallway and seen clearly in the last panel. The picture in question is "The Reward of Cruelty" by William Hogarth, the final piece in Hogarth's series, "Four Stages of Cruelty." Various writers, including Stephen Knight and Jean Overton-Fuller, have repeated claims that the illustration, while ostensibly a satirical portrayal of then-current medical practices, is in fact an exposition of Masonic ritual murder techniques for those who knew how to read the clues. Both Knight and Overton-Fuller point out striking similarities between the mutilations in Hogarth's picture and those carried out on the victims of the Whitechapel murderer, which seemed to me to give the picture in question at least enough resonance to justify its inclusion here.

PAGES 17 & 18

This domestic scene featuring Marie Kelly and her live-in lover Joe Barnett is inverted, although most books on the subject quote Joe Barnett as mentioning Marie Kelly's seemingly inordinate obsession with the Whitechapel murders in the weeks leading up to her death. According to *The JTR A-Z* by Begg, Fido & Skinner, many of Kelly's friends also spoke of Marie's seeming terror concerning the murders and her desire to leave London.

PAGES 19 & 20

The scene here is an invention based upon speculations by various authors upon the sexuality of Prince Eddie and his close association with his Cambridge tutor, J.K. Stephen. The details regarding the Cambridge society known as "The Apostles" are taken from *The Ripper Legacy* by Martin Howells and Keith Skinner (Sidgwick & Jackson, 1987). The poem quoted by Stephen here, entitled "A Thought," is reproduced in Dr. David Abrahamsen's *Murder & Madness, The Secret Life of Jack the Ripper* (Robin Books, 1992), amongst other places.

PAGES 21 & 22

The fact that the inquest into the death of Catherine Eddowes was handled by the City Police rather than by the Metropolitan police due to the location in which her body was discovered is common to most of the Ripper literature. The dialogue during this sequence has been taken where possible from transcripts of what was said during the inquest, quoted in this instance from *JTR, Summing Up And Verdict* by Wilson and Odell. The fact that Elizabeth Stride was buried in pauper's grave No. 15509 in East London Cemetery is as according to *The JTR A-Z* by Begg, Fido and Skinner.

PAGES 22 & 23

The scene between Abberline and Emma depicted on these pages is an invention for story purposes. As noted before, there is no reason to suspect that Frederick Abberline enjoyed even the most innocent of relationships with any East End woman.

PAGE 25

The information concerning Sir Charles Warren's farcical bloodhound experiment, along with the illustration shown in the last panel, are as according to *The Ripper File* by Melvin Harris (W.H. Allen, 1989).

PAGES 26 - 28

The information that Sir Robert Anderson had urged the incarceration of every streetwalker in the East End for her own good comes from *JTR, The Uncensored Facts* by Paul Begg, while the information regarding the questioning of Richard Mansfield, leading actor in the stage production of Jekyll and Hyde, comes from *The Complete Jack the Ripper* by Donald Rumbelow (W. H. Allen, 1975), as does the information about Herbert Freund, arrested for causing a disturbance at St. Paul's cathedral. Robert Lees' account of his supernatural visions is as related in Knight's *JTR: The Final Solution*, while the frosty reaction of the police to Lees' offer of occult assistance is as reported by most sources that mention Lees involvement. The only alteration that I have made to the scene is the implication that Lees may have been deliberately attempting to lead the police to William Gull in order to briefly embarrass and discomfit a man that he felt had

snubbed him, as suggested in my appendix notes for page twelve of this current episode.

PAGES 29 & 30

The details of Annie Chapman's inquest on the eleventh of October are as found in Begg's *JTR, The Uncensored Facts* and *The JTR A-Z* by Begg, Fido and Skinner. Whether Inspector Abberline indeed attended as depicted here is not recorded. The dialogue relating to John Pizer and his somewhat suspicious arrest at the hands of Sergeant Thick is for the most part accurate according to inquest records, although Pizer's mutterings as he leaves the court are based upon my own conjectures.

PAGES 31 - 33

These pages present a necessary fiction to cover the authorship of the "From Hell" letter received by Vigilance Committee leader George Lusk on October 16th. Gull's reference to having formally preferred the work of Goethe but having become more inclined towards Dante in his later years are according to *William Withey Gull, A Biographical Sketch*, although the interpretation of this change of preferenceis my own.

PAGE 34

This account of the receipt by George Lusk of the "From Hell" letter and human kidney are according to *The JTR A-Z* by Begg, Fido and Skinner.

PAGES 35 & 36

Godley's reference here to Dr. Winslow having received a remarkably prophetic letter stating that the next murder would occur on November eighth or ninth is supported by references in

Wilson and Odell's JTR, *Summing Up And Verdict*, although I confess that I'm currently at a loss as to where I got the name "Lunigi" from. I know it's in one of the books that currently surround me in teetering mounds, but its precise whereabouts remain elusive. Either take my word for it or come round and do my housework for me.

The scene on page thirty-six needs a little explanation. Scotland Yard received dozens, perhaps hundreds of letters purporting to come from the killer and rendered in a variety of handwriting styles. The fact that one man was actually killing and disemboweling prostitutes at this time almost pales into insignificance beside the fact that lots of ostensibly normal men through-out the country were fantasizing about doing the very same thing. Lest this be seen as evidence that men alone harbour such dark notions, it should be pointed out that Godley's reference to the only convicted hoaxer being female is accurate. Her name was Maria Coroner and the brief outline of her case is detailed in *The JTR A-Z* by Begg, Fido and Skinner. She is the only author of a "Jack the Ripper" letter that can be positively identified.

P A G E S   37 - 40

The suggestion that a row occurred between Marie Kelly and Joe Barnett on the thirtieth of October, during which Kelly broke a window, is raised by Paul Begg in JTR, *The Uncensored Facts* amongst others books on the subject. Barnett's stated reason for the rift with Kelly was that she was inviting other prostitutes home to sleep in their room at Miller's Court, notably a woman named Julia. The sexual element of the quarrel is my own interpretation of Barnett's remarks, but is probably not unlikely in light of the fact that many prostitutes, for fairly obvious reasons, choose other women for their recreational relationships. It also seemed plausible that someone living under the shadow of her own impending murder might embark upon a reckless last bout of unbridled hedonism in the brief period of time left to her.

P A G E S   41 & 42

The scene depicted here is an invention based upon the fact that Marie Kelly apparently lost her front door key in the week or two imme-diately prior to her murder. Most of the books on the Whitechapel murders mention this fact, but the one closest to hand is *The JTR A-Z* by Begg, Fido and Skinner.

P A G E   43

The return of Prince Eddie to London on the first of November, before continuing to Sandringham on the second of November, is according to Court Records as quoted in *The JTR A-Z* by Begg, Fido & Skinner. The suggestion that Gull was treating the prince for syphilis, in which the doctor specialized, is according to various sources, including *Clarence* by Michael Harrison (W.H. Allen, 1972).

P A G E S   44 & 45

The scene on these pages is an invention, although for the benefit of American readers I should perhaps point out that "bonfire night" is a reference to the fifth of November, when the execution by burning of Guy Fawkes is celebrated by burning effigy figures in his memory. Fawkes was one of the conspirators charged with attempting to blow up the House of Parliament in the seventeenth century.

PAGES 46 - 48

The scene depicted on these pages is an invention, save for the detail of Marie Kelly and Maria Harvey waking together on Wednesday the seventh of November, which is according to *The JTR A-Z*, as is Marie's purchase of a halfpenny candle at McCarthy's shop next to the entrance of Miller's Court in Dorset Street.

PAGES 49 & 50

These pages are based upon the testimony of Thomas "Indian Harry" Bowyer, an Indian army pensioner who worked for Marie Kelly's landlord, John McCarthy. On the Wednesday night in question, Bowyer reported seeing Marie Kelly standing in Miller's Court with a man of "perhaps 27 or 28 [who] had a dark moustache and very peculiar eyes. His appearance was rather smart and attention was drawn to him by showing very white cuffs and a rather long white collar, the ends of which came down in front over a black coat. He did not carry a bag." This is quoted from Paul Begg's *JTR, The Uncensored Facts*. My decision to make Prince Eddie the person described is largely based upon the aptness of the description. The prince was 24 with the required moustache and peculiar eyes. He was also known by the nickname of "Prince Collars-and-Cuffs" because of his habitual dress, which involved long white collars to mute the effect of his swan neck, along with rather prominent cuffs. Given that it suited

my story purposes to have Marie Kelly made aware at this juncture as to the precise date of her impending death, I decided to make the guilt-stricken prince into the bearer of the bad news.

PAGES 51 & 52

The description of Marie Kelly being visited by one Lizzie Albrook on the afternoon of Thursday the eighth of November is according to Albrook's testimony as recounted in *The JTR A-Z*, as is the gist of their conversation together.

PAGE 53

Warren's resignation as commissioner, formally accepted and announced on the ninth of November, is reported in all of the books on the subject. Supposedly the result of a long series of difficulties between the commissioner and the home office, the fact that Warren resigned on the day of the last Ripper murder is apparently as coincidental as the resignation of Assistant Commissioner James Monro on the night before the first murder. So nothing suspicious there, then. The reference to the Lord Mayor's Show (which took place upon the morning of the ninth) as an important event in the Masonic calendar is according to Stephen Knight, who also suggests that the killer might have chosen the date for this very reason.

PAGE 54

Joe Barnett's visit to Marie Kelly in Miller's Court is based upon the testimony of both Lizzie Albrook and Joe Barnett, as related in *The JTR A-Z* by Begg, Fido and Skinner. The suggestion that Kelly and Barnett may have visited the Horn

O'Plenty public house for a drink with "Julia" later in the evening is according to the evidence of one Maurice Lewis, as documented in the same source.

PAGES 55 - 58

The events on these pages are a reconstruction of various eye-witness accounts (all to be found in *The JTR A-Z*) relating to Marie Kelly's last night. She was seen with at least two different customers during the evening, taking them back to her room to conduct trade. The exchange between Marie and her neighbour Mrs. Cox depicted here, along with Marie's rendition of "Only a violet plucked from my mother's grave" are accurate according to Mrs. Cox's testimony, and the second man seen entering Miller's Court with Marie is as described by one George Hutchinson. Hutchinson reports a detailed conversation with Marie, but along with other students of the case I find something rather unconvincing about the amount of detail and tend to suspect that much of it was invented after the fact by a man eager to place himself at the centre of attention. In any event, the depiction of Marie's second visitor is a sop to Hutchinson's testimony, even if I didn't consider the man worthy of a walk-on part.

For those interested in the timing of events, it is estimated that the killer probably took Marie Kelly's life a little before four in the morning. This was the time given by Elizabeth Prater, who lived directly above Kelly. Prater said that it was shortly before 4:00 A.M. when she was awoken by her pet kitten walking over her neck. (Isn't that a frightening little detail?) Upon awakening, Mrs. Prater heard cries of "murder" issuing from somewhere outside, but since such cries were common in the East End, she ignored them and went back to sleep.

Appendix to continue in future volumes of *From Hell*.